Little Mouse's Birthday Cake

Thacher Hurd

HarperCollins*Publishers*

Little Mouse's Birthday Cake
Copyright © 1992 by Thacher Hurd
Printed in the U.S.A. All rights reserved.

Library of Congress Cataloging-in-Publication Data
Hurd, Thacher.
  Little Mouse's birthday cake / by Thacher Hurd.
      p.   cm.
  Summary: Disappointed that his friends seem to have forgotten
his birthday, Little Mouse goes skiing by himself.
    ISBN 0-06-020215-7. — ISBN 0-06-020216-5 (lib. bdg.)
    ISBN 0-06-443353-6 (pbk.)
    [1. Mice—Fiction.   2. Birthdays—Fiction.]   I. Title.
PZ7.H9562Lm   1992   91-11919
[E]—dc20   CIP
                                                           AC

Little Mouse looked out his window.
It was winter.
The ground was covered with fresh snow.

Today was Little Mouse's birthday.
Little Mouse wondered—Would his friends
have a party?
Little Mouse thought, "Perhaps they forgot. I will
call them."

Little Mouse called his friend Gloria.
"Are you busy today?" Little Mouse asked.
"Um…" said Gloria, "…actually, I'm doing something today."
Gloria didn't say anything about Little Mouse's birthday.

Little Mouse called his friend Chip.
"Are you busy today?" Little Mouse asked.
"Oh, I was just going out the door to do something important," said Chip.
Chip didn't say anything about Little Mouse's birthday.

Little Mouse called his friend Chuck.
"What's up?" said Little Mouse.
"Can't talk now," said Chuck. "I'll call you tomorrow."
But tomorrow would be too late.
Little Mouse's birthday would be gone.

Little Mouse thought, "I don't care. I'll just go skiing and forget all about it."

Little Mouse put on his mittens and his jacket and his ski boots. He put on his backpack and went outside.

It was a beautiful winter day.
Little Mouse decided to climb Mouse Mountain and
ski down.

It was hard work climbing Mouse Mountain.

Little Mouse stopped on the way up and drank some
hot chocolate.

Finally, Little Mouse made it to the top.
The view was magnificent. Little Mouse sat for a long
time, gazing into the distance.

Little Mouse imagined that he was sitting on top of a
giant birthday cake.

The sun was getting lower in the sky.
Little Mouse put on his skis. He looked over the edge.
It was steep.
Little Mouse pushed with his poles, and—

WHOOOOSH! He whizzed down the mountain.

Little Mouse went faster and faster.
Suddenly, Little Mouse took a tumble.

When he came to a stop, Little Mouse didn't know
where he was. There were trees all around, and they
all looked the same to Little Mouse.

Little Mouse started to walk.
Then he stopped to listen. It was quiet in the woods.
The sun was going down.

Perhaps he could see where he was from up in a tree.
Little Mouse scrambled up a big oak.

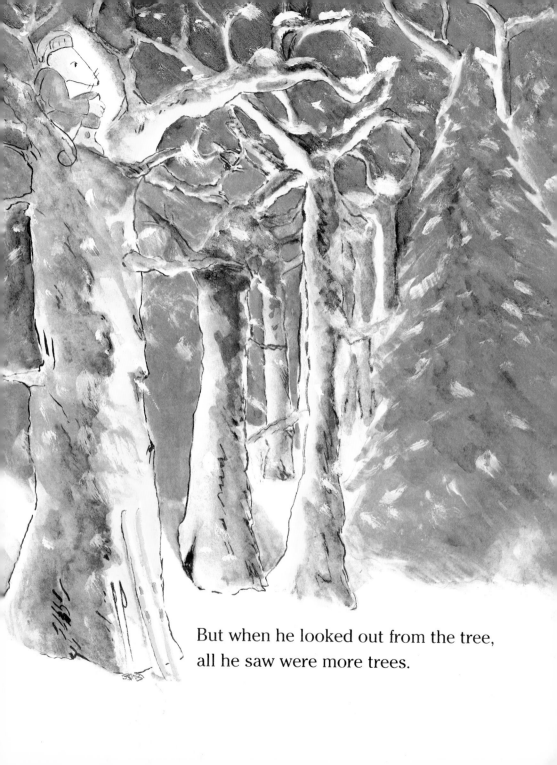

But when he looked out from the tree,
all he saw were more trees.

Little Mouse pulled his hat down around his ears and buttoned up his jacket.

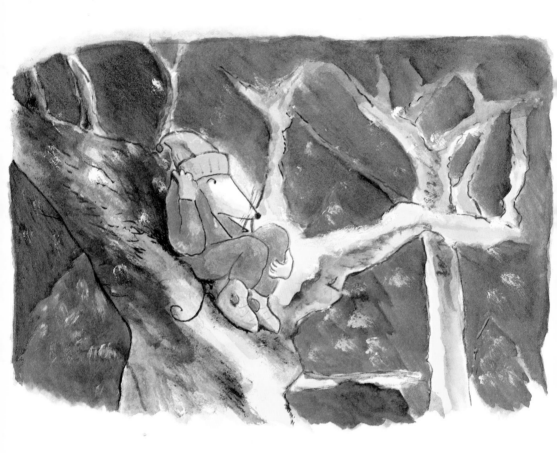

He snuggled into the crook of the tree.

Little Mouse closed his eyes. Soon he was asleep.

Little Mouse dreamed about a pink birthday cake. It was rolling down the mountain toward Little Mouse.

But just as the huge birthday cake was about to land
on Little Mouse's head, he woke up.

Far away, Little Mouse heard someone calling his
name. "Little Mouse!"
In the distance he saw flickering lights.
Little Mouse called back, "Hey, over here!"

It was Gloria and Chip and Chuck.

"How did you know where I was?" asked Little Mouse.

"We followed your tracks," said Gloria.

Gloria and Chip and Chuck smiled up at Little Mouse.

"Are you going to spend all night up in that tree?"
said Chuck.

Little Mouse climbed down out of the tree and strapped on his skis. Gloria led the way as they skied through the forest.
Soon they came to the edge of the woods.

There below them was Little Mouse's house.
They skied down the hill in the moonlight.

Gloria smiled at Little Mouse when they got to his
house.
"Cover your eyes," she said, as she opened the door.

"Golly!" said Little Mouse.

"YUM!" said Little Mouse.
"I made it myself," said Gloria.